This edition produced for The Book People Ltd, Hall Wood Avenue,
Haydock, St Helens, WA11 9UL

First published in hardback in Great Britain by HarperCollins Publishers Ltd in 1997
First published in Picture Lions in 2000
3 5 7 9 10 8 6 4
ISBN: 0 00 762434 4

Picture Lions is an imprint of the Children's Division, part of HarperCollins Publishers Ltd

The HarperCollins website address is: www.**fire**and**water**.com

Manufactured in China

THE OWL'S LESSON

NICK BUTTERWORTH

TED SMART

Swallows and swifts flew high above the head of Percy the park keeper. Soon they would be off on their long winter holidays. Some birds had already gone.

Percy was thinking how nice it would be to join them, but his thoughts were soon brought back down to earth.

"Percy! Look what we've found!"

Just ahead of him, a squirrel friend and the mole were standing over a heap of twigs.

"Hello," said Percy. "That looks like an old nest." He picked it up. "I shouldn't think anyone lives in it now."

"Then you'd be wrong," said a little voice. A small feathery head stuck itself out from beneath the twigs. "I live in it. And you're holding me upside down."

"I'm so sorry," said Percy. He turned the nest over. "I thought you would have gone with your friends and relations."

"Can't fly," said the little bird. "I didn't get the hang of it."

"Oh dear," Percy began, but he wasn't allowed to finish.

"Good morning!"
It was the owl.

"Owl!" called Percy. "Can you help?
This little fellow can't fly."

"Flying?" said the owl, as she swooped
overhead. "Nothing to it," she hooted,
as she went into an impressive spin.
"Just flap and go!"

The owl shot up into the air and out
of sight. Almost at once, she was back
again, flying just above their heads.

"You see," she cooed,
    "it's easy..."
"Look out!" shouted Percy...

THUMP! The owl hit a pine tree. Pine cones rained down on the squirrel and the mole,

followed by the owl in a dazed and untidy heap.

"Well," said Percy, "I think there's a lesson for us all."

"Percy," said the squirrel, "have you got any string?" Percy felt in his pocket.

"Here's a piece," he said. "Why do you want it?"

The squirrel jumped to his feet. "Come on," he said to the little bird. "I'll give you a piggy-back."

Percy looked puzzled as the squirrel began to climb a tree with a very nervous passenger on his back.

"He needs to get used to heights," explained the squirrel.

W hen he reached the top, the squirrel tied the string between two branches.

"It's a tightrope," he said. "Follow me!"

Balancing carefully, the squirrel stepped onto the string. The little bird bravely followed.

"Hooray!" cheered the mole.

"Well done!" called Percy. "We'll have you taking to the air in no time."

At that very moment, with a twang! one of the squirrel's knots came undone and the tightrope walkers found themselves falling.

The squirrel managed to grab the end of the string. The little bird didn't. As he looked down, he expected to see the ground rushing towards him. Instead, he saw Percy, holding out his cap.

The little bird fell right into Percy's cap, but so hard, that he bounced straight out again.

"Oh no!" shouted Percy. "He's going to fall into those thorn bushes. Fly! Fly!"

And, as if he'd been doing it all his life, that's just what the little bird did. He flew. Away from the thorns, up into the air and perched at the top of the tree.

"Don't stop," called the owl.
"You can go after your friends
and relations now."

The little bird looked delighted.

"I will!" he called back.

"Thank you everybody!"
and with that he was off
over the tree tops.

"Don't mention it," said a voice dangling from a piece of string halfway up a tree. "Don't mention it."

Nick Butterworth was born in North London
in 1946 and grew up in a sweet shop in Essex. He now lives
in Suffolk with his wife Annette and their two children,
Ben and Amanda.

The inspiration for the Percy the Park Keeper books
came from Nick Butterworth's many walks through the
local park with the family dog, Jake. The stories have sold
over two million copies and are loved by children all
around the world. Their popularity has led to the making
of a stunning animated television series, now available on
video from HIT Entertainment plc.

Read all the stories about Percy and his animal friends . . .

then enjoy the Percy activity books.

And don't forget you can now see Percy on video too!